P9-DBY-345

DOG DIARIES

BARRY

DOG DIARIES

DOG DIARIES

BARRY

BY KATE KLIMO • ILLUSTRATED BY TIM JESSELL

RANDOM HOUSE 🏠 NEW YORK

The author and editor would like to thank Marc Nussbaumer,
curator, Natural History Museum, Bern, Switzerland, for his
assistance in the preparation of this book.

This is a work of fiction. All incidents and dialogue, and all characters with the exception of
some well-known historical and public figures, are products of the author's imagination and
are not to be construed as real. Where real-life historical or public figures appear, the
situations, incidents, and dialogues concerning those persons are fictional and are not
intended to depict actual events or to change the fictional nature of the work. In all other
respects, any resemblance to persons living or dead is entirely coincidental.

Text copyright © 2013 by Kate Klimo
Cover and interior illustrations copyright © 2013 by Tim Jessell
Photographs courtesy of the Natural History Museum, Bern, Switzerland, pp. 142–144

All rights reserved. Published in the United States by Random House Children's Books,
a division of Random House, Inc., New York.

Random House and the colophon are registered trademarks of Random House, Inc.

Visit us on the Web! randomhouse.com/kids

Educators and librarians, for a variety of teaching tools, visit us at
RHTeachersLibrarians.com

Library of Congress Cataloging-in-Publication Data
Klimo, Kate.
Barry / by Kate Klimo ; illustrated by Tim Jessell. — 1st ed.
pages cm. — (Dog diaries ; #3)
Summary: Barry der Menschenretter, a Saint Bernard dog, reflects back on his life in the
early 1800s at the Hospice of the Great Saint Bernard in the Swiss Alps, where he rescued
some forty people from avalanches. Includes facts about the breed and the hospice.
ISBN 978-0-449-81280-8 (pbk.) — ISBN 978-0-449-81281-5 (lib. bdg.) —
ISBN 978-0-449-81282-2 (ebook)
1. Saint Bernard dog—Juvenile fiction. [1. Saint Bernard dog—Fiction. 2. Rescue dogs—
Fiction. 3. Dogs—Fiction. 4. Avalanches—Fiction. 5. Hospice du Grand-St-Bernard
(Bourg-Saint-Pierre, Switzerland)—Fiction. 6. Alps, Swiss (Switzerland)—History—
19th century—Fiction. 7. Switzerland—History—1789–1815—Fiction.]
I. Jessell, Tim, illustrator. II. Title.
PZ10.3.K686 Bar 2013 [Fic]—dc23 2012047455

Printed in the United States of America

10 9 8 7 6

First Edition

Random House Children's Books supports the First Amendment
and celebrates the right to read.

For Alan Armstrong, who likes big dogs
—K.K.

The courage and steadfastness of dogs
to their duty is hopefully inspirational
to their two-legged partners.
—T.J.

CONTENTS

LITTLE BEAR

My name is Barry der Menschenretter. That's
MEN-shun-RET-tuh. A big name, you say? Well,
in life, I was a big dog. If you want to see me with
your own eyes, go to the Natural History Museum
in Bern, Switzerland. There you will see my stuffed
body in a glass case. I apologize in advance for my
appearance. They repaired me and patched me and
added fur and stuffing in 1923, raising my head to
show me in a less humble pose. In spite of all their

efforts, I no longer look very much like myself. But perhaps you can see something of the original dog in me if you look carefully and imagine.

I come from a long line of big dogs called mastiffs. Mastiffs marched and fought with the Roman army in ancient times. Even before that, there were mastiffs in a faraway place called Tibet. In modern times, my kind of mastiff is called a Saint Bernard, but in the year 1800, when my story begins, there were no such things as Saint Bernards. Dogs such as I were called *Alpenhunde,* a German word that means "dogs of the Alps"—the high mountain range in Switzerland, a country in western Europe. People also called us butchers' dogs, perhaps because we ate so much meat every day that only a butcher could afford to keep us.

But the most common name for us dogs was bari. *Bari* means "little bear" in Swiss German.

That's what my name means: Little Bear. With my thick fur and big, padded feet—like a bear—I was well suited to living in the cold.

The place in the Alps where I lived is so high there is snow on the ground almost all year long. It is 8,000 feet above sea level. During your time, people have learned to master the snow. They plow through it in vehicles with special wheels and shovels. They fly over it in silver birds called airplanes. They even play in it, sliding down it on sleds and on skinny sticks called skis. In my lifetime, before special vehicles or skis, snow was a very serious matter. In fact, where I came from, people called snow the White Death.

Today, there is a tunnel bored through solid rock that is a shortcut from one side of the Alps to the other. But in my day, there was no tunnel. People who needed to get from Switzerland to

Italy had to climb over the Alps on foot or ride on mules. When the steep mountains got buried in snow, the going became difficult—and sometimes impossible. Almost as bad as the snow were the swirling banks of fog. People froze. They got lost. They got buried alive in avalanches.

What is an avalanche? An avalanche is a great big spill of snow, rocks, and ice that comes thundering down a mountainside as if some giant has sent it tumbling. Avalanches are unpredictable things and have many causes. Sometimes when the temperature rises there is a sudden thaw, causing wet, heavy snow to slide. Other times, a new layer of fresh snow slips down the face of an older layer of snow. However it comes about, if you happen to be standing in the way of an avalanche, you are out of luck. There is no time to escape.

That is where we baris came in. Our job was

to guide the lost, to warm up the frozen, and to find those buried alive. In my lifetime, they say I rescued over forty travelers from the White Death. They say I was a hero. But I say I simply loved the snow. I loved to walk in it. I loved to roll in it. I loved to search for people buried under it. If it is heroic to do what you love—and to do it well— then I guess I was a hero. But I prefer to think of myself as a Dog at Home in the Snow.

Let me tell you a bit about my home. It was a big, plain stone building called the Great Saint Bernard Hospice. In those days, a hospice was a place where weary travelers could stop and rest before moving on. My particular hospice was named after Bernard de Menthon, the cleric who founded it almost one thousand years before I was born. A cleric is a man of the church who has taken a vow to help people. Bernard's special mission was to help travelers in their trek along the steep mountain paths—to guide them when they were lost and to feed them and warm them when they were hungry and cold.

In those days long ago when Bernard was still alive, people who crossed the mountains had to deal not just with snow, but with robbers, too. Bernard believed travelers should have shelter from the weather and protection from robbers. For hundreds of years, the clerics of the Great Saint Bernard Hospice carried out the wishes of their founder. But it was only in the 1700s that we baris arrived at the mountain.

Baris came to live at the hospice when some noblemen gave us as gifts to the clerics. It was lonely and desolate up there. Not many people wanted to live in such a high, windblown, snowy place. The noblemen thought the clerics could use the company. One of the things we baris are very good at is snuggling. We are big dogs with big hearts. We also make very good guard dogs, not because we are vicious, but because we are big and discouraging to robbers.

But the clerics soon discovered that we dogs are also very good workers. Hitch a bari to a sled and he or she could haul a load of firewood much more easily than a cleric could. A bari could go from the town of Bourg-Saint-Pierre up to the hospice with as much as thirty pounds of supplies strapped on to its back. The clerics and their worldly helpers, the marronniers (mah-ron-ee-AY), began to take us out with them on their twice-daily patrol of the paths in search of people lost in the snow. They soon discovered that the travelers were much less likely to lose their way in heavy snow, sleet, or fog with a bari leading them.

In my day, there were twenty clerics and marronniers living in the hospice with eight dogs. Day in, day out, a steady stream of travelers passed through. Travelers who came to the hospice received cheese and bread to eat and wine to drink.

They were able to hang up their wet clothes to dry.
Wrapped in blankets, they sat and toasted themselves before a roaring fire in the refectory. If they
stayed the night, they could sleep in a small, pri-
vate room or in the dormitory on a bed with clean

sheets and warm blankets. And if they needed it, they got a dog and a marronnier to guide them through the pass, which followed along the ridge that lay between two of the highest mountains of the Alps: Mont Blanc and Monte Rosa. It was a busy, lively place—a good place for a dog. There were always new people to meet, new scents to sniff, and important jobs to do.

I was born one late spring day in a big room in the cellar of the hospice where the clerics kept the casks of wine. It was dark and damp down there, but it was home to us. It's the place where we dogs slept and ate and had pups. I had a brother, Jupiter, and a sister, Phoebe. Mother was very proud of us. In those first few weeks, we stayed with Mother in the cellar. Father was gone much of the time, and when he did come back, he flopped into the corner and slept.

My legs were still shaky and my eyes were barely open when I first started making my move toward the door. I had watched the big dogs as they opened the door with their muzzles and disappeared. I wanted to sneak out behind them and see what was on the other side. But before I ever had a chance, Mother would pick me up in her mouth by the scruff of my neck and bring me back to the corner, next to the casks. The corner was where she kept us in a nice clean bed of straw and rags.

But I want to go out and see the world, I told Mother as I squirmed to free myself from her gentle jaws.

You will get to do that soon enough, Mother said, plopping me down next to my brother and sister. *When you're bigger.*

I am big enough now, I grumbled. I was three

weeks old and already too big to fit in Michel's hat. Michel was the marronnier in charge of taking care of us.

I like it here, said Jupiter, snuggling up to Mother's teat. *We get to snuggle and drink warm milk whenever we want it.*

And we also get to listen to the clerics sing, said Phoebe.

Phoebe was right. From where we were in the cellar, we could hear the clerics singing every day, once in the morning and again in the evening. Their voices drifted down from the chapel. It was a sound to stir a dog's heart. But I wanted more. I wanted to be like the big dogs. I wanted to go where they went and do what they did.

One early morning, I woke up blinking and shivering. Even with the warm bodies of all the sleeping dogs, it had gotten cold in the cellar. There were chinks in the wooden door. I lifted my nose to them. My nostrils quivered. Somewhere beyond the door, I smelled something cold and dry and very big. What was it?

Mother was dozing while Jupiter and Phoebe suckled.

I butted Mother's big head softly with my nose. *Mother?* I whispered.

Mother lifted her muzzle and yawned. She had a big, wide mouth and a long pink tongue. *What is it, my puppy one?* she said, nuzzling me.

I smell something, I said. And my nose twitched almost as if it had a will all its own.

That is dog and straw and milk and mud that you smell, my darling puppy boy.

I shook my head. *No, it's something else.* I lifted my nose to the door again.

Then the clerics began to sing, and the sweet

sound made me sleepy. I dropped my head onto my paws and drifted off. When next I lifted my head, I heard a roaring, whistling sound.

I wagged my tail and said to Mother, *What is happening?*

Mother twitched her nose and sniffed. *It is a blizzard,* she said. *You smelled it even before it came. That's a very promising sign.*

Jupiter and Phoebe stood up and shook out their hides.

What is a blizzard, Mother? Phoebe asked.

A blizzard is a great deal of snow blown hard by the wind from out of the sky, Mother said.

What is snow? I asked.

What is wind? Phoebe asked.

What is sky? Jupiter asked.

Such curious little puppies I have! You'll find out the answers to your questions soon enough, Mother

said. She gathered us to her big, warm side and snuggled us. *Right now your place is here with me. Latch on and drink your fill of milk. Get big and strong so you can go out in the snow.*

While we were talking, I noticed that the older dogs had gotten up, shaken out their coats, and nosed their way out the door.

Where are they going, Mother? I asked.

They are going out into the blizzard to see if people need help in the snow, she said.

I want to go out into the blizzard and help people in the snow, I said.

She laughed softly. *If you went out now, Barry, you could not even help yourself. You would sink into the drifts. I would have to dig you out and pick you up and carry you back inside by the scruff of your puppy neck. You must wait until you are bigger. Then you can go out in the snow.*

That afternoon, Father came in. His eyes were red and he looked very tired. I smelled the blizzard on his coat.

He circled three times and flopped down on the floor, heaving a huge sigh. I went over to him and took his ear in my mouth and tugged. His head was bigger than my entire body. *Where have you been, Father?* I asked.

He opened one eye. *You would not believe it if I told you,* he growled.

Oh, tell me, tell me! I begged.

Father opened the other eye and began to speak in his deep, rumbling voice. *There are more travelers on the path than I have ever seen,* he said. *Thousands of them. They are all dressed alike and are dragging cannons that they have placed inside hollowed-out tree trunks. Today, I saw one of the cannons slip off the ropes that held it and plunge over the mountainside into the gorge. Six soldiers and your cousin Juno went with it. Yesterday, some of the men and cannons were stuck in the crevasse. It took many hours to haul them out. We dogs helped. It was hard work. The men were very cold. The cannons were very heavy.*

What are cannons? I asked.

Cannons are big, heavy metal tubes that shoot hot, searing fire, Father said. *The men are called soldiers. The soldiers use the cannons to fight other soldiers in battles in the lands far, far below us.*

I knew what a battle was. I fought battles every day with my brother and sister over who was going to get to suck Mother's juiciest teat. Sometimes we bit each other. Sometimes we kicked each other. Sometimes we punched each other in the face with our paws. But as much as I loved our mother's milk, I could not imagine using something like a cannon to fight against my brother and sister. That would hurt!

Father went on. *Prior Louis does not approve of the soldiers. He says the battle is madness. But he will let some of the soldiers stay in the hospice. Others will camp out in the snow.*

Prior Louis was the leader of the hospice. His word was law.

You mean the soldiers are coming here? I asked.

Father nodded and closed his eyes. He started snoring almost right away.

I lifted my nose to the door and smelled something new. I did not know it then, but the scent I had picked up was gunpowder. And it smelled dangerous!

2

THE LITTLE COLONEL

In the house above me, I heard the hospice come alive. Doors slammed and boots clomped and loud voices laughed and sang and shouted. I smelled meat cooking. Mother had told us that one day we would be eating this wonderful-smelling stuff instead of drinking her milk. My mouth watered. I was ready to eat that meat right now!

Suddenly, the door swung open. Michel stood there in his heavy coat. He liked to spend time with us pups. He would sit by our nest and let us crawl over his lap.

"Venus," he whispered to my mother, "you must get ready to have your puppies handled."

My mother sighed and gathered us toward her.

The next moment, another man came into the cellar. He wore tight trousers and a long jacket and carried a hat with a feather under his arm. He was not as tall as Michel.

"So this is where you keep the remarkable dogs," said the stranger. "But why so few of them? Where are the others?"

"The other dogs are all out in the snow rescuing your soldiers, Your Excellency," said Michel.

"Ah, yes, very good," said the visitor. He ambled over to our corner. Mother looked up at the little man and growled long and low.

"Heh-heh. These great big dogs don't look so

very big to me," said His Excellency.

"These pups are only a few weeks old," said Michel. "They will be big soon enough."

"I will eat now," said the little man, and he turned and walked out the door.

Michel rolled his eyes as he followed the man out of the cellar. "The Little Colonel must be fed," he muttered under his breath.

Later, I learned from listening to the clerics and the marronniers speak that the man Michel called Excellency was known far and wide as Napoléon Bonaparte. He was the leader of the country of France, but it was not enough for him to lead France. This little man wanted to lead all of Europe. So he set out to conquer it with his army. That was why he had ordered his soldiers to drag the cannons over the mountain to Italy. To his face, they called him Excellency. But behind his back, just as Michel had done, they called him the Little Colonel.

The Little Colonel is dangerous, Mother said as soon as he had left the room. *He reminds me of the small dogs I have seen in the company of travelers. They need to convince the world that they are big dogs. They bark and bite and growl ferociously. That Napoléon is a small dog trying to act like a big one.*

A few days later, one of the Little Colonel's officers came down to the cellar. We saw right away that he had a kind face and a gentle voice.

"Hello, good Mother Venus," he said as he bent down over us. "I am General Berthier, and I would be honored to hold one of your magnificent puppies."

Instead of growling as she had at the Little Colonel, Mother pushed me toward the general.

He gently picked me up with his rough hands.

My stomach dropped as I felt myself rising high up into the air. He smelled like damp wool and sweat and gunpowder. He scratched me beneath the chin and behind the ears. I licked his fingers. They tasted good and salty.

"You're an armful already, aren't you!" the general said. "And very friendly, too." I wagged my tail and looked up at him. I was not old and wise like my mother, but I saw that this man had eyes like Michel—eyes a dog could trust. "Good Mother, do you mind if I take your pup for a little stroll around the hospice? I've been out in the cold for so very long. Holding this warm bundle of fur in my arms will offer great comfort."

I looked down at Mother, expecting her to demand my return immediately. But instead, she said, *Barry, go with the nice man and tour the hospice. Behave yourself and come back soon.* Then she showed him her soft eyes and let him know that it was all right to take me.

Goodbye, Mother! I'm off to see the world! I said as the man draped me across his arm. He took me through the door and up to the hospice. Right away, there was so much to see. The halls were long and narrow and crammed full of what had to be soldiers. Each man put one hand to his head when he saw the general. As the general walked by, some of the soldiers petted me. We passed through a room where men sat with their long legs stretched out. They held small square things in their hands and tossed silver pieces down on a table. Every few minutes, one would slap down the square things and say, "I win!" The others shouted some words I didn't understand, but Mother later said they were words a tender, young puppy was not meant to hear.

We walked past the game-playing soldiers and through another door. My nose twitched. I smelled food. We seemed to be following its scent. The general was a man after my own heart. The scent was delicious. I licked my chops. We soon found ourselves in a room Mother had told us about. It was the kitchen. It was the place where all food, even dog food, was prepared.

The shelves groaned beneath bags of beans and flour and rashers of bacon. Slabs of meat and whole ducks and chickens hung from the ceiling. There was a big iron stove where pots of soup and stew boiled and gave off heavenly clouds of steam. One-handed, the general helped himself to a cup of stew. Some of it splashed on his wrist, and he let me lick it off. It tasted even better than Mother's milk. While he ate, we watched the fireplace, where a large roast skewered on a spit dripped into the flames. Old Luc, one of the most senior dogs, was hitched to a big round wheel. He walked in a slow circle. As he walked, the spit holding the meat turned slowly over the fire.

I looked down at him and said, *You must grow*

dizzy walking around and around like that.

Old Luc looked up at me and ran his tongue over his sagging jowls. *This is not as hard as it looks, little one. And after I have turned the spit and the meat is cooked, they will give me a heel of bread dipped in the juices. It is the best.*

"The clerics have devised a very clever contraption here," the general said to a nearby soldier. The soldier, a tall, skinny lad, stood watching the meat with hungry eyes.

"These big dogs have many talents," said the soldier. "I watched one of them save the life of a man today. We had been marching through the snow for hours and my friend could not go another step. He staggered and fell into a snowdrift. You should have seen him. He looked so peaceful, as if he were settling down for a nap. But I know that's how we freeze to death. I was too weak to lift him up, and ice had begun to form on his face. His breath was slowing. Then one of the dogs came along. She licked the ice off his face and kept licking until the soldier woke up. I watched as the dog grabbed his hand and pulled him to a seated position. After a bit, my friend came to his senses and took to his feet. But that dog kept an eye on my friend until we came to the hospice. If it weren't for that dog, Napoléon's army would have had one less soldier. That's a cute puppy you have there. But one day that puppy will perform miracles like the rest of them."

"Is that true?" the general said, scratching me on the back. I wagged my tail and licked his fingers. *Give me a taste of what's on that spit and I'll perform a miracle right now,* I growled.

The general laughed. He held me in his arms all that evening as he went around the hospice and visited his men. Some of them were in bed, exhausted from the trek up the mountain. Others lounged by the fire. Still others sat around the table in the dining hall and ate and drank and grumbled about the folly of dragging guns across the Alps. But all of them spoke of the bravery of the dogs. Hearing this made me feel very proud to be one of them. Many men petted me and chucked me under the chin and fussed over me.

Late that night, the general sat with me by the fire in the refectory. I shrank back from the red and orange tongues of flame.

The general said, "That's fire, my little pup. It cooks meat, but it also warms bodies. It won't hurt you so long as you don't get too close to it. It will also make you drowsy."

Other dogs had come in from the cold. They shook out their coats. Then they lay down on the hearth, soaking up the warmth from the fire.

I don't mind the soldiers, said the dog named Marius. *But I do mind the guns.*

I was just beginning to fall asleep in the general's snug, warm lap when Michel's voice awoke me.

"There you are!" he said. "Venus is beginning to worry about her little pup. And I am sure that by now you must be missing her, too."

Now that I thought of it, I did miss Mother. I liked the general, the warmth of the fire, and all this attention, but I was hungry! The general let me gnaw on his big finger, but there was no milk to be had there.

"I have so enjoyed holding this puppy," the general said to Michel. "All of your dogs are so well behaved and friendly."

"They are happy in their work," said Michel.

"What would you say to my buying this pup?"

said the general. "I think he would fit in very well with Napoléon's army, don't you?"

Michel had been friendly with the general until that moment. Now I glimpsed a coldness in his eyes that rivaled the blizzard outside.

Michel clicked his tongue. "Barry is far too young to be taken away from his mother," he said.

"In that case, I would be happy to wait a week or two until he is old enough to be separated from her," said the general.

"These dogs are not for sale. The hospice needs as many dogs as we can get. We lost a dog today, in fact, when one of your cannons went over the edge of a cliff, and another was buried in an avalanche last week. We can't afford to lose a third." Michel held out his arms for me.

The general sighed. "I understand." I could sense his reluctance to let me go. But he handed me to Michel. I think he sensed the marronnier's displeasure. "I want to thank you for your gracious hospitality and for letting me hold Barry. He and all the dogs have made us weary soldiers feel very much at home."

Many of the soldiers were very happy there with us, up on our mountain. So happy was one of Napoléon's generals that the Little Colonel later had his body taken to the Great Saint Bernard Hospice to be buried. Whenever I saw his tomb, I would stop and sniff and remember the soldier with the kind face and gentle voice who wanted to buy me. I marvel at what a different sort of life I would have led had I gone away with the general and the Little Colonel to fight in battles. Instead, I remained at the hospice and grew up to fight a lifelong battle against the White Death.

SNOW

One morning, Michel came down to the wine cellar to fetch me and my brother and sister. He clapped his hands. "Come along, puppies. Come with me! You're going outside!"

We scrambled after him, tripping over our big paws. We were big now, two months old. I came up almost to Mother's knee.

Have fun, children! Mother called after us. I think she was secretly happy to be rid of us. By then, we had begun to eat food instead of drinking her milk. The cellar was getting too small to hold us. We spent our days romping and snarling and battling each other. We were excited and ready to get up and go.

We followed at Michel's heels, up the stairs, along the hall, down the steps, and out the front door into the great wide world!

Phoebe and Jupiter tumbled out the door, but I stood on the sill. *Wait just one moment,* I said slowly, looking around. I wanted to give myself a chance to take it all in—the sights, the scents. I did not want to rush headlong into this new world.

Wait? Who wants to wait? There's so much to see! Phoebe said as she followed a black beetle until it disappeared down a hole. There were smaller ones just like it in the cellar. This one was big!

Jupiter was staring at a little brown creature sitting on the top of a scrubby bush. The next we knew, the thing flew up in the air and flapped away. Jupiter ran after it, barking. *Hey, where do you think you're going?* he hollered.

"Come back, Jupiter," said Michel, laughing. "That bird is a ptarmigan. Be nice to it."

I joined Michel at the bush. I liked it. I had a friendly feeling toward it. I lifted my leg and did what came naturally to us dogs. My piddle ran down the bush's twigs and soaked into the ground.

I shook myself and stopped to look around. The bush and the bird were all very fine. In the distance I saw a row of rocky crags. There was a wide blue expanse of water down below. But something was missing. I looked up at Michel, sat down on my haunches, and whined far back in my throat.

"What's the matter, Barry?" said Michel. "It's a beautiful summer day in the mountains and, for once, there's not a patch of snow in sight."

My point exactly! Where is the snow? I had waited all my young life to see the snow and now it was nowhere to be found. What was the meaning of this?

"Don't worry, Barry," said Michel. "Enjoy the mild weather while you can. The snow will be here before you know it."

And that is what Phoebe and Jupiter and I did for the next few weeks. Every morning, after the clerics had finished singing, we followed Michel outside into the hospice yard. We played out of doors all day long. We sniffed the wind. We barked at the brown ptarmigans. We chased the furry, fleet mountain hares. We rolled in the grass. And when we weren't chasing hares or birds, we were chasing

each other up one slope and down another, our playful yips and barks echoing off the rocks of the pass.

At the end of each day, Michel would appear at the door of the hospice and call us. Then we would come running. One day when Michel called us, I did not come. I was busy stalking a hare. I had my nose to the ground, following the trail of scent the hare had left. I went around and around and finally I came to a chink in the rocks.

"Barry!" Michel called.

The hare was beneath those rocks. I knew it. I poked my nose into the hole and got a powerful whiff of hare. *Sorry, Michel, but I am busy with a hare just now,* I growled, never taking my eyes off the hole. My thought was: *Michel will understand.*

But Michel did not understand. "Barry!" he said again in a very stern voice. "I don't care what you are doing. When I call you, you will come. That is what we call obedience."

I gave a snort. What was obedience? Was it a hare? Was it a bird or a beetle or a nice bush twig to chew on? What did I care about obedience?

The next thing I knew, Michel was standing over me. He reached down and grabbed me by the scruff of the neck, just like Mother did. I was a big dog now, coming up almost to my mother's shoulder, but he picked me up all the same. He was strong!

"Barry, you will stop whatever you are doing and come to me when I call," he said. He shook me, not hard, but just enough to get my attention. Then he dropped me. I fell in a furry heap. His face was cold and angry.

I put my tail between my legs and looked up at him, and my expression said, *I am all for obedience,*

Michel. From now on, when you call, I will come.

And I did. Whenever I heard Michel or any of the other clerics or marronniers calling my name, I came. Michel and the others were always so happy to see me that I was glad I had.

Toward the end of the summer, I noticed that my fur coat was getting thicker. I wondered why that was. Then one early morning, while it was still dark outside, I found out the reason. I was in the cellar, fast asleep, when something made me open my eyes. Everything was silent, quieter than I had ever heard it. Has that ever happened to you? That a silence, rather than some noise, wakes you up in the middle of the night?

I went over to the door and sniffed between the cracks. I smelled snow. While the other dogs slept on, I got up and pushed through the door. I ran up the cellar stairs, along the hall, and down the front steps, my claws scritch-scratching on the stones. When I came to the front door, I lifted a paw and banged at it. Brother Henri came. It was his turn to stay by the door all night to greet travelers who might arrive. "Are you ready for your first snow, Barry?" he whispered, grinning.

He opened the door and let me out.

How can I describe what it was like to see the world I knew—the hospice, the storage sheds, the rocky walls of the pass, the meadow where my brother and sister and I had played all summer, the bush, even the lake—all cloaked in a layer of pure white?

And the silence! We dogs have very sharp ears. But as the snow fell, it made no sound at all. I leapt off the porch and immediately slid onto my rump. This snow was slippery stuff! It was wet and slick like the floor after the clerics had finished mopping

it. It was cold, too. Even through my thick coat, I
felt that it was colder than the water from the lake.
I stood up, making an effort to keep all four legs
beneath me. I put out my claws and grabbed on

to the snow. I walked a little way. Then I couldn't resist a second longer. I dropped down and rolled on my back in the snow. How can I describe it? It was bliss.

After a while, Brother Henri called me back inside and I came running, because I am an obedient dog. I went back down into the cellar and fell into a deep sleep. I was exhausted after my first encounter with the cold white stuff. I dreamed I was chasing hares through the snow.

When I woke up, I knew it was still snowing. It was cold in the room. The older dogs were getting up and shaking themselves.

It's snowing again, Old Luc said, heading for the door.

Those travelers will not rescue themselves, said Bernice, following him out.

Can I come, too? I asked.

Not until you have learned how it's done, said Bernice. *You would only be in the way.*

All day long, as men and dogs came and went, guiding travelers who had gotten lost in the snow, I stood by the door and watched. Never had I felt so left out. That evening, as I was settling down after my dinner, Michel came to visit me. He was wearing his thick woolen coat and his furry hat. He had a long stick in one hand and a lantern in the other.

"Are you ready to learn to walk in the deep snow, Barry?" he asked.

He did not need to ask me twice. I wagged my tail and followed him out the door. Earlier, the snow had not been this deep. I could tell by how Michel's stick sank into the whiteness that it was twice as deep as I was tall. I remembered Mother telling me that I would sink and have to be dug out. So I hesitated on the step.

Michel stepped onto the snow. He didn't sink. His big, flat boots held him up. Perhaps my paws would do the same for me. I set a paw onto the snow. It sank. I pulled back. Then I widened my paw and set it down. My splayed paw stayed on the top of the snow. I tried that with my other paw, and soon I was standing with all four feet on top of the snow!

"Come along, Barry," said Michel, setting out. "We're going to take a nice moonlit walk."

I followed Michel. The light from his lantern sparkled on the snow. But soon I was leading the way. Could it be that my sense of smell guided us along the path more surely than the lamplight? The little bush was buried in the snow. Only the rooftops of the sheds showed. When I turned to look back at the hospice, I saw drifts of snow that nearly reached the second story. In the valley below, the lake was covered with a crust of white. My breath steamed in the air. Did I feel the cold? Yes, but it didn't make me shiver. It made me feel *alive*!

In spite of the heavy blanket of snow, I could still smell the earth far down below. I could smell the hares burrowing and the bugs and the plants asleep in the dirt. I still had the scent of the path in my nose, and of all the feet that had trod over it for so many years that no dog—and very few men—could keep count. Every so often, I would halt and sniff and make sure that the path was still beneath me. Sometimes I ran quite a way ahead, but I never lost track of Michel. His tall, slender figure cloaked in black with the pointed cap was easy to see against the stark whiteness of the snow.

Every evening, when he had finished singing in the chapel, Michel took me out to walk. I quickly learned that the hares that were brown in the summer were now white. They skittered over the drifts, nearly invisible to my eye. White, too, were the once-brown ptarmigans. But my own coat did not turn all white. I kept my brown spots. And my fur, though thicker, was still short. This was good because the snow did not form little balls on it as it did on the coats of the longer-haired dogs that sometimes visited the hospice. Those poor dogs got cold and stayed cold.

One fine night, I was padding along in the snow in front of Michel when I came to a sudden halt.

I could not have said what stopped me like that. Perhaps it was a stillness in the air and the earth, even more arresting than the stillness of the snow. Michel stopped, too. He swung his lantern toward me.

"What is it, Barry? Are you dawdling tonight?" he asked. He was not angry with me. But he was curious. I was curious, too. Something was happening. Something in the earth that came up through my feet and filled my body with the force of its presence.

Something was coming! Something huge and heavy and cold!

Suddenly, ahead of us, a good distance away but close enough that we could see it, a great rumbling torrent of snow came rushing down the mountainside. The silence was filled with a mighty thundering that shook the earth. Michel called out and turned away to hide his head behind the collar of his coat.

Then the thundering stopped and the earth grew still again. I no longer recognized the way ahead. It was buried in a deep layer of fresh snow.

I confess that I could not help myself. I whimpered and cowered. Michel shook the snow off his cloak, then bent down and hugged me.

"You will be all right, boy. You have just witnessed your first avalanche," he said.

And I knew with every bone in my body that it would not be my last one, either.

HIDE-AND-SEEK

More avalanches followed. When the avalanches hit, the older dogs—Old Luc and Marius and Father—would go to the front door to wait while the clerics got ready. The clerics put on their cloaks and hats and took their long sticks in hand. Then the dogs would lead the way out into the snow with the clerics following behind, dragging their long sleds.

I would wait anxiously by the door. Sometimes

I waited all day for them to come back. Once Marius returned alone. He barked and barked.

We need more help! he said.

Is it bad? I asked.

Some men are trapped in an avalanche! Marius said. He panted from the long run.

What will you do? I asked.

Brother Martin and Brother Gaston came to the door.

"What's wrong, Marius?" asked Brother Martin.

Marius grabbed Brother Martin's hand in his mouth and pulled.

Brother Martin looked at Brother Gaston and said, "It seems we are needed."

Brother Martin, Brother Gaston, and two mar-ronniers donned their heavy cloaks and got their long sticks. I said to Marius, *What's happening out there? Tell me, what do you do when you go out on a mission?*

You will find out soon enough, Barry, Marius said.

The brothers went outside and each drew a sled from out of the shed. They followed, one after the other, in Marius's paw prints. I stood in the yard and watched until all five of them disappeared into the whiteness.

I sighed. I was nearly full-grown. Why couldn't I go with them?

Someone stroked my head.

I looked up into Michel's kind face. "What is the matter, Barry? Do you feel left out?"

I whimpered. Michel understood me so well.

"Your first birthday is coming soon. Your time to take part is nearly at hand," he told me.

I was still waiting by the door when I spied the

rescue party in the distance. On each sled was a body bundled in black wool blankets, bound by ropes.

Michel and others inside the hospice sprang into action. I stood by and watched, trying to stay out of their way but wishing I could do something to help. They heated big pots of wine on the fire. They got heaps of blankets and dry clothes ready. In the kitchen, the clerics on duty prepared a thick savory soup. They filled two big basins with water and ice and snow. *What was that for?* I wondered. The hot wine and dry blankets and soup I could understand. But surely the travelers had had quite enough of ice and snow!

By the time the rescue party drew their sleds up to the door, everyone inside the hospice was ready. Two marronniers went outside to help. They lifted two of the men from the sleds and carried them into the sitting room. Two of the men were able to get up and walk with the aid of a cleric on each arm. The clerics walked these men around and around in circles. Then they sat them down before the fire. Michel and Brother Martin knelt and took off the men's boots and rubbed their feet. A marronnier who worked in the kitchen brought each man a goblet of hot wine. The travelers sat and sipped the wine and sighed with gratitude. As I stood near the fire and watched the two travelers, I saw the color return to their faces. I wagged my tail. One of the men smiled, reached out, and stroked the fur on my back.

"Thank you," he said.

Why thank me? I had not done anything. Perhaps to him, all of us dogs looked alike. But this was good news, yes? This meant that I was getting big enough to go out in the snow and rescue travelers. I felt the excitement coursing through my body.

Then I turned to see what was happening with the other two men. The marronniers had stripped off all their clothing. How pale and still their bodies looked. That worried me. Then I watched in astonishment as the clerics lowered them into the basins of ice and snow!

One of the men began to shout and splash about. The blue of his body grew pink and rosy. He sputtered. I think he was angry with the marronniers for dunking him in the cold water, and I cannot say that I blamed him. But the marronniers just smiled. They helped him out of the basin and toweled him off and dressed him in dry clothing. Then they led him to bed.

Meanwhile, the other man just lay in the basin of ice and snow, his eyes staring up at the rafters. Michel looked at Brother Martin and they shook their heads. They lifted his body out of the ice and wrapped it in a blanket and carried it back into the snow. Outside of the hospice, there was a special building where the marronniers brought the bodies. The cold kept them fresh until the ground was soft enough to bury them or their families came to claim them and bring them home.

The White Death had claimed one of the men, but the other three had been spared.

Two months later, I was one year old. On a spring day when the snow was deep, Brothers Martin and Gaston took me out for a walk in the snow. I stopped and looked back at the hospice.

Where is Michel? my eyes asked.

Michel was my special walking companion.

"What's the matter, Barry?" Brother Gaston asked. He exchanged a secretive look with Brother Martin.

"Come along, Barry," said Brother Martin as he set off briskly in the snow.

Though disappointed not to have Michel at my heels, I took the lead and ran down the path. It was the path that ran south toward Italy. Brothers Gaston and Martin followed along behind me, poking their long sticks into the snow as they walked.

We were only a short distance away from the hospice when suddenly I smelled something familiar. The scent was coming from a bank of snow a little way off the path. I stopped and tested the air with my nose.

I knew what I smelled.

It was Michel! But where was he? I could not see him. I spun around and looked. There was nothing but snow everywhere. I ran all over the bank of snow with my nose to the ground, my tail between my legs, sniffing frantically. I ran in a wide circle. As the smell grew stronger, the circle shrank. Finally, I stopped and lifted my head. I barked loudly to call the brothers over. They were some distance away from me.

"What is it, Barry?" Brother Martin called out.

"I think our furry friend may have found

something," Brother Gaston said.

They struggled toward me through the drift, poking their sticks into the snow. They were so slow! I could not wait another moment. I started digging. After a while, behold, there was Michel's pale face, looking so very cold! My friend was buried in the snow! I licked his face, his hands. I looked over at the brothers. Wasn't one of them going to go back and get the sled? Weren't they going to bring Michel back to the hospice to warm him up and give him hot wine and soup and dry clothes and blankets? I licked and licked my friend until the pinkness bloomed in his skin.

But what was this? Michel was laughing! Brothers Gaston and Martin had begun to help dig him out, and they were now laughing, too! As far as I was concerned, this was no laughing matter. Michel had been buried alive in the snow. I stared

from face to face. Brother Gaston needed to blow his nose, he was laughing so hard. Brother Martin wiped tears of laughter from his eyes.

"Oh, Barry!" Michel said. "The look on your face!"

Then it was as if the clouds rolled away and the sun beamed down on my head. I understood! This was what the older dogs did when they went out on rescue missions. They sniffed around in the snow and found people buried in it. This was a test. Did this mean the brothers thought I was ready to go out in the snow and rescue people?

When Michel emerged from the snowbank, he leaned down and wrapped his long arms around me and hugged me hard.

"Barry, my fine young dog," he said, "it appears that you have a nose for finding people in the snow!"

THE WHITE DEATH

The second winter of my life it snowed very hard, but that did not discourage people from making the trek over the mountains. All sorts of reasons drove people to take this trip. There were merchants who carried their goods in heavy packs strapped to their backs. There were farmworkers and their families traveling to pick crops. There were others going to visit friends. But no matter how much snow fell, they all kept coming.

Each morning and afternoon, one marronnier headed south down the path toward Italy. A second headed north toward the valley of the Rhône River. Their job was to search for travelers who might have gotten lost in the snow or who were too cold to continue. There was a cave just off the northern path where travelers stopped to rest. The marronnier was always careful to check the cave. They brought a dog or sometimes two with them. Even though I was a young dog, I liked to go out on my own. Michel permitted this because he had seen that if there was someone lost in the snow, I would find them.

Why was this? you ask. As Michel had said, I had a nose for the work. Even if the wind was against me, I could smell a human being up to two miles away. I could smell a man buried under many feet of snow. And I could sense well in advance when an avalanche was coming.

One day when I was about four years of age, I was patrolling the route on the way to Italy when I smelled men nearby. I could not see them anywhere, so I wandered off the track and soon came upon a group of them carrying bundles on their backs. Unlike me, they were not able to find their way by smelling what was beneath the snow, and they had wandered off the path. I guided them back in the right direction. They seemed dazed from the cold. It was my opinion that, for their own safety, they should return to the hospice, which they had left that morning.

"He wants us to go back to the hospice," said the loudest-voiced man, who seemed to be the leader, "but we cannot lose another day. We are already late with our delivery. Sorry, dog, we aren't going that way."

"Well, I, for one, will never make it to Italy without another night of warmth," said another. He was so cold his teeth chattered in his head.

They argued until the cold man won out over the leader. They let me take them back to the hospice. While we walked, they grumbled. They complained of hunger and weariness and cold.

"When will we reach the hospice?" the Cold Man said.

I knew it was only a short distance away. I kept making tracks through the snow, until suddenly, I stopped. The men halted behind me.

"The dog stopped. Why is the dog stopping?" the Leader asked.

"Come on, dog," said the Cold Man. "You

wanted us to go to the hospice. Let's get there before my tongue freezes in my head."

I did not move. I had stopped because I sensed something coming. Something Big. And I knew, as surely as my name was Barry, that if we kept going in the same direction, this Big Something was going to bury us alive. I turned around and went the other way. When the travelers refused to follow, I barked at them to show that I meant business.

"This is crazy," said the Leader. "We've made a decision to go back to the hospice and that is where we should go. We can't go around in circles like this."

"I don't know," said the Cold Man. "The dog seems to be wary of something. These dogs have a reputation for being very smart. I'm going to play it safe and follow the dog."

The men stood in the snow and argued while I

whined. What was the matter with them? The Big Something was coming and we needed to be gone from this spot. There was no time to lose.

When they stopped arguing, two of them had decided to follow the Leader back to the hospice. The Cold Man and two others followed me away from it. I had done what I could.

We had walked for about fifteen minutes when we heard it behind us: the roar of a mighty river of snow and ice and rocks as it rushed madly down the mountainside toward the valley. I knew that the avalanche had probably overtaken the three who had not heeded my warning.

The three in my care jabbered and wept and prayed for the lives of their companions. They also knew that had they not followed me, they would now be under the snow. I turned around and set off in the direction of the hospice. The path now lay buried in debris. The air was filled with a fine film of snow and dust. The men were nowhere to be seen. I took off at a run, leaving the three survivors on the site while I raced to get help. When

I got to the hospice, I barked and barked until I summoned two marronniers from their chores.

"I have the feeling that Barry has found some avalanche casualties," one of them said. "I am betting it is the party who left here this morning."

Brother Gaston, Michel, and Brother Martin got their cloaks and sticks and followed me, dragging the rescue sleds. Bernice and Jupiter came, too. I would need their help to find the bodies buried in the snow. Fortunately, the avalanche was not so very far away from the hospice and we arrived in less than an hour. The three survivors cried out when they saw us. Brother Gaston wrapped them in blankets and sat them on one of the sleds while we dogs set to work.

We ran in circles, our noses to the rubble brought down by the avalanche. I was the first to catch the scent. I stopped and barked. Michel came over and poked his stick far down in the snow. He stopped when the stick was about half buried. The stick would sink no farther. It appeared that it had hit something solid. It might have been a rock, but I had a feeling that it was a man. I wagged my tail.

"Good work, Barry," Michel said to me.

My chest swelled with pride. It made me happy to please the clerics and the marronniers.

"He is down about six feet," Michel said to the others.

They got their shovels from the sled and began to dig away the snow. I helped with my paws. Meanwhile, Jupiter and Bernice continued to sniff for the other two men. By the time Jupiter started to bark, we had dug the Leader out of the snowbank.

He spat snow out of his mouth. Then he looked at me, his breast heaving. "I should have listened to you, dog. You were right and I was wrong."

The clerics hustled the man over to the sled, laid him out, and bundled him in blankets. Then we went over to where Jupiter stood barking. Again Michel poked his stick down in the snow. The stick sank almost entirely.

"He is buried very deeply," said Brother Martin with a hopeless shrug.

My brother and I dug along with the clerics until finally we uncovered the man at the bottom of the pit of snow. To everyone's amazement, he was still breathing. The clerics lifted him and laid him on the snowbank. While they went to fetch the sled, I stretched myself out next to the man and warmed him with the heat of my body. Jupiter licked his face. By the time the clerics had gotten him onto the sled, his eyes were open. He was blinking hard, but he could not yet speak. Later, at the dinner table, his tongue would loosen enough to speak of this brush with the White Death as if he were the hero of the tale instead of a fool who hadn't listened to me.

Bernice was standing some distance down the mountainside from us. She was barking fit to burst.

She had found the third traveler. It looked as if the avalanche had carried him halfway down to where the mountainside dropped off into the valley below, and where the snow that had come down in the avalanche mixed with gravel and big boulders. Could a man survive such a tumbling and tossing? Bernice's bark had a note of bleakness to it. Jupiter and I whined. We knew what that bark meant and so did the clerics.

When we dug up the man, life had already left his body. But as the clerics struggled to bear him up the mountainside to the sled, they were as gentle with the body as if he were still alive.

On another occasion, I woke up one morning and ran up to the top of the stairs. Out the window, I could not see the crags of the pass. At first, I thought it was because of snow. But the air in the hospice felt warm. And then I knew. It wasn't snow. It was fog. I had seen fog but never fog this thick. I scratched at the front door. There were bound to be travelers lost in a fog as thick as this.

Brother Gaston let me out. "Don't get lost in the pea soup, Barry!"

I ran along the path. There were pockets of fog so deep I could not see beyond the end of my muzzle. The fog was filled with smells that confused me. If I did not keep my nose to the ground, I would lose my way, too. The fog was quiet. It was like a big white blanket that lay across the shoulders of the mountain.

Suddenly, I heard voices. The voices did not sound worried at all. They were singing. I followed the sound. I went off the path and in a downhill direction. I did not like the direction the voices were taking me.

I came upon two travelers walking along with heavy packs strapped to their backs.

"Look!" said the taller of the two travelers. "It is a bari dog come to rescue us."

"Hello, bari dog. It is good to see you, but as you can tell, we are not in need of rescue," the shorter of the two said.

I begged to differ. I clamped my mouth around the wrist of the taller man and pulled and tugged at him.

"What are you doing, dog? Leave me alone!" he said, trying to wrestle his hand back. But I would not let go.

"Maybe there is something wrong with the dog," the Short One said.

The Tall One snorted. "Maybe we should get out our gun and shoot the crazy cur in the head."

Just then, a breeze came along and parted the

fog long enough for the travelers to see exactly where they stood.

At the edge of a sheer drop.

The Tall One staggered away from the edge of the precipice. His foot dislodged a rock. The rock went over the side. It was a long time until we heard it land, far, far below us in the valley.

The two travelers stared at each other. That rock might have been one of them!

Then another breeze came along and the fog was back.

The two travelers huddled next to me.

"Show us back to the path, dog," they begged. "We need your help."

I gladly led them up the slope and back onto the path. Needless to say, there was no more talk of shooting me. It was "good dog" this and "smart dog" that from then on. And when I delivered them to the hospice door, they patted me on the head and offered me a piece of dried meat from one of their packs. I took my reward and went back out into the fog to see if there were any other travelers who might have been lost in its swirly depths.

In the years to come, I rescued others from the fog. I have to say that I preferred working in snow. With snow, you always knew where you stood. But fog confused even me sometimes. It made things that were far away seem close. It fooled my nose and it fooled my ears. Fog was a trickster.

THE PROMISE

One winter's day when I was six years old, I woke up with a bad feeling in my gut. I thought I might have gotten a piece of spoiled meat in my dinner bowl the night before. I was not one to complain, but I felt I should let Michel know that I was not feeling like my usual self. I went to where he sat polishing some boots by the fire.

He set down his boots and looked at me carefully. "What is it, Barry?" Then he saw that the light in my eyes was dull and my tail was tucked between my legs. With gentle fingers, he felt my nose. It was dry and warm.

"Feeling a little under the weather, Barry?" he asked.

I might have said that. Even my droopy ears felt like they drooped more than usual.

"What do you think about taking a nice walk in the snow?" he asked. I managed to wag my tail once or twice, although I never really got it going. He took my feeble wag as a *yes* and got his cloak and stick.

I know it might sound strange to you. When you feel sick, the last thing you want to do is take a walk in the snow. But for a dog like me, a walk in the snow was, as I believe the saying goes, exactly what the doctor ordered. The first burst of cold air hitting my face was like a soothing balm. It did not entirely restore my health, but I did feel better. Thoughtful fellow that he was, Michel had chosen the path that headed north so the winds whipping up from the south would not hit us head-on. I trudged along beside my friend instead of bounding ahead in my usual eager manner.

We entered a small valley. The hospice was well out of sight by then. We climbed down one side and were just climbing up the other when the wind died down and the world turned quiet and still. Too quiet and too still. I stopped and did not move a muscle.

Michel said, "You're tired, Barry. Let's return to the hospice. I can see this wasn't such a good idea after all."

He started to go back down into the valley, but I grabbed the sleeve of his cloak in my teeth and held him there. I growled. My eyes said, *Heed me,*

Michel, and do as I say. Do not go down into the valley.

Michel looked surprised. "It's not like you to growl at your old friend Michel. You really aren't yourself today, are you?"

Not true! My sickness was all but forgotten and I was as much myself as ever. I knew one thing and one thing only: we must not go into that valley. Something was coming, and it was coming very soon. Michel tried to get me to release my hold on him, but I would not. If I did, he might go into the valley. And I could not let that happen.

Then we heard rumbling like thunder in the crags above us. Michel's eyes widened and he stared at me. He understood. Michel threw himself on the ground next to me and wrapped an arm around my neck. The very next moment, an avalanche came crashing down into the valley.

When the earth had settled, Michel sat up and smiled at me. "You must be feeling better, eh, boy?" he said.

I stood up and shook the snow out of my coat. He stood up and brushed the snow off his cloak.

Just then, we heard the bells of the chapel ringing. Michel said, "Well, I guess it's safe to go back to the hospice now. They will worry that we were caught in the avalanche. Let's go and calm their fears."

But I was not going anywhere. Something beckoned to me, something farther down the path in the direction we had been heading when the avalanche hit.

Michel grew weary of trying to coax me to go back. "Well, Barry, my furry friend," he said, "I am sorry to say that I am cold and I have duties back at the hospice. I am returning now."

But I knew that I would wander as far as I had to go to track down the scent that tugged at my nose. The snow was deep and the wind was strong, but finally, I came out of the valley and onto level ground. I knew now where the scent was leading me: to the cave in the northern mountainside.

When I arrived at the cave, I found a woman.

We did not get many women on the mountain. But I knew one when I saw one. She was bundled against the cold and huddled up against the back of the cave. She looked cold and very weak. I went over and licked her, but her face remained as pale as ice. Then she rolled aside, and I saw that in the shelter of her body lay a little boy, not much bigger than a baby. When the woman moved, she must have wakened him. He whimpered and reached out for her. In weak and shaking arms, she gathered up the boy and held him out to me.

"Lick my son, bari, and keep him warm," she said as she set the wee lad on the cave floor before me.

I licked the boy's face and hands. He squirmed, but I wouldn't let him get away from me. I lay down next to him and gave him my biggest, warmest bari hug. He soon calmed down. He knew he needed the warmth of my tongue and my furry body.

Then the woman slowly hoisted herself up on one elbow. She removed the red shawl from around her shoulders.

"Roll over on your side, bari," she told me.

Obedient as I was, I rolled over next to the small boy. With the shawl, the woman bound the boy on to my back. She tied the shawl so tightly it was difficult for me to breathe, but I understood she wanted to keep her boy securely tied to my back. "There. See that no harm comes to him," she said.

I stood up slowly with my new burden on my back. It was difficult, carrying such a load. I was unsteady at first, but I managed to find my balance.

The woman looked up at me. "Promise me you will carry my boy to safety," she said.

I barked softly and leaned down to lick her face. It had worked wonders on the son; perhaps it would work on the mother. But I could tell that life left her body even as I nuzzled her. Now it was just the boy and me.

I turned around and walked out of the cave with my precious burden tied to my back. I was a strong dog but I was no mule. It was not easy carrying a wriggling toddler. The weight shifted as I walked, and I had to move to keep my body beneath the boy's. If he came off my back, I might not have been able to get him to the hospice without dragging him there. And dragging him might hurt him even worse than the cold.

I stopped to rest frequently, leaning my body against a boulder or a tree. I dared not lie down lest I find myself unable to get up. There were times when the boy went so still that I worried the life might have left his body, too. When he coughed or began to stir again, my heart soared. I trudged along all through the night, and as dawn lit the sky, I heard the peal of the chapel bells. The hospice was close now, but I had to move so slowly and so carefully that it might as well have been on the other side of the mountain.

When I came to the valley, I followed Michel's tracks down one side and up the other. At the top of the rise, I could see the smoke from the hospice's chimney. I headed toward it, slowly but steadily. I came into the hospice yard and leaned against a shed to catch my breath.

Never had I been so tired. But I had kept my promise to the dying mother. I had brought her child to safety. Still, I worried. Would the boy survive after all this time in the bitter cold?

While I was resting, I heard someone call my name.

It was Prior Louis. I recognized him by his long black cloak and his peaked hat with the tassel on the top. He came over from the hospice, leaning on his long stick. "We were just about to send out a

search party for you, Barry! Where have you been? We were so worried."

I walked toward him, weaving.

"Barry, are you hurt?" he asked, coming to my aid. "And what is wrong with your back?"

When he came close enough, he saw that apart from weariness, there was nothing wrong with me. But there was a small boy tied on to my back with a red shawl.

"What is this?" he cried. He leaned over and untied the shawl. He lifted the boy in his arms.

The boy was silent and still.

Prior rushed him into the warm hospice kitchen. I followed close at his heels. I had gotten the boy this far. I was not about to let him out of my sight now.

Prior spread out the red shawl and laid the boy on the table, next to a pile of onions and potatoes.

Other men came into the kitchen. They crowded around the table. I poked my nose between them to see what was going on.

"He's not breathing," said Prior.

I did not like the sound of that. Breathing kept people and dogs alive. What were they going to do about this? I felt better when Michel burst into the room. The others made way for him. He leaned over the boy and rubbed his limbs and his narrow chest.

The boy coughed and began to whimper.

The men cried out with joy. I wagged my tail. The boy was alive!

They wrapped the boy in blankets and took turns holding him. They should have let the boy lie down next to me. I would have kept him warm with my bari hug. But wherever they took him, I followed. I knew that my place was at his side.

Michel looked down at me and said, "Don't worry, Barry. We are taking good care of your boy."

They had better be taking good care of him! I had made a promise to his mother that no harm would come to him. I watched while they spooned hot soup into his mouth. I watched when they put him onto a cot.

"Come eat something, Barry," said Michel. "You have worked hard and you must be starving."

But I lay down next to the cot. If the boy woke up, I wanted to be the first thing he saw.

Michel brought my food, and I ate it there next to the boy. When he woke up, I saw that he had beautiful eyes, the color of a summer sky. He smiled and reached out a small pink hand to pat my nose. I licked him for good measure, and he threw his arms around me.

I stayed with the boy as much as I could. When

his legs regained their strength, I toddled with him up and down the halls. Together we explored the hospice and the grounds. I showed him all my favorite places, like the bush and the corner of the cellar where I was born. I introduced him to my brother and sister and to all the dogs.

When the spring came, a woman and a man came up from the valley to take him to a new home. I sniffed their hands.

"Will I do, Barry?" the man asked me.

I snorted and wagged my tail. He would do. He smelled right. The important thing was that the boy seemed to like them. As he rode off down the mountain in a mule cart, I stood at the door and never took my eyes off him until he was out of my sight. Before he disappeared down the dip, he smiled and waved. The wind carried his voice to me. "Bye-bye, Barry!"

7

MICHEL LOST

In the winter of my eleventh year, it snowed a great deal. Sometimes the snow was so high, the drifts reached the second-floor windows of the hospice. How strange to look out the windows and see a blue wall of snow pressing up against the glass. We dogs worked harder that winter than any time in memory.

I had formed a routine with a couple of the other dogs who worked well with me: Jupiter and a two-year-old—a real up-and-comer—named Artemis. Artemis had an excellent nose on her. The three of us would go out into the snow together on our own and patrol the roads. Sometimes we went north toward the valley of the Rhône River. Sometimes we went south toward Italy. If we found travelers who were lost in the snow or who had wandered off, we led them back to the path. If they were overcome by the cold, one of us would run back to the hospice to get help while the other two stayed and kept the travelers warm.

Two of us dogs had a way of lying down on either side of a freezing-cold traveler so that we formed a living blanket. In this way, we would keep the cold person warm until the clerics arrived on the scene with the sled and blankets. During that winter alone, we rescued six people from the White Death. But before the winter was out, I would encounter the biggest challenge of my lifetime.

We had just come back from a particularly difficult rescue mission. We had found a husband and a wife and their baby buried in an avalanche. We worked hard to bring the family back to life. They were buried deeply, and the snow was wet and heavy and difficult to move. There is an old expression, *dog tired.* That day, I knew what it was. Every bone in my body was exhausted. As I lay with my head on my paws, Michel came to me and nudged me gently with his boot.

"Don't tell me you are too tired to take a walk with me today," he said.

I opened my eyes and looked up. Michel was already in his coat and fuzzy hat. He seemed eager and full of energy. Just looking at him made me feel tired. I let out a long, shuddering sigh.

"It seems you are too tired. I guess I am on my

own today. I will see you later, Barry," he said as he took his stick and set out alone.

I slept a deep, dreamless sleep for most of the afternoon. When I woke up I shook myself out and went to look for Michel. I searched the sitting room. There were travelers by the fire. But no Michel. I searched the kitchen. There were clerics preparing a delicious-smelling roast and vats of steaming soup, but there was no Michel there, either. I searched the hallways and dining room and the dormitories and even the chapel and the stable. But there was no Michel anywhere in the hospice or on the grounds.

I trotted over to Prior Louis's study and bumped my nose on the door. Prior Louis opened it. He looked out. I could tell he was expecting to see a person standing there. I pawed at the floor to get his attention.

He shifted his glance downward. "Oh, hello, Barry," he said. "Was there something that you wanted?"

I am worried, my eyes told him.

Prior Louis must have been in the middle of doing something very important, for he returned to his desk. He took up his pen and began to make squiggly marks on the paper.

I stood beside him at the desk. I began to whimper. Prior Louis kept writing. It made a scratchy sound. Then I put my paw up on his knee.

I am worried sick, my eyes told him.

Prior Louis put down his pen and sighed in an exasperated fashion. "Barry, can't you see that I am busy?"

Just then, Brothers Martin and Gaston appeared in the doorway.

"What is it, Brothers?" Prior Louis said.

The brothers bowed their heads respectfully. Brother Martin said, "Pardon the interruption, Father, but we are worried. Michel went out alone for a walk hours ago and he has not yet returned."

Prior looked down at me, understanding dawning on his face. "Was that what you were trying to tell me, Barry?" he asked.

Finally! I sighed.

"Of course," said Brother Martin softly. "Our Barry always knows whenever something is amiss."

The prior rose quickly from his desk. "You must go and search for our lost man," he said. His brow was wrinkled, and now he looked as worried as the rest of us were.

I waited while the brothers got ready to go out into the snow. They lit lanterns and donned their heavy cloaks and hats and drew two long sticks from the stack by the front door. As soon as the

door opened, I bolted and bounded across the snow. Michel was out there somewhere. And I had to find him!

Nose to the ground, I followed Michel's trail. Concentrating fiercely, head low, tail high, I followed his scent along the path he had taken earlier. As I went, a bad feeling in my gut grew, and this time I knew it had nothing to do with what I had eaten.

Darkness had fallen by the time I came to the place where Michel's tracks dropped off the edge of the path into a steep gorge. Dogs and men alike avoided this dangerous spot. I descended into the gorge. I could tell from the jumbled look of the snow that Michel had not walked. He had tumbled. And it was a very long tumble down to the bottom of the gorge. When I got to him, his face, in the light from the moon, was blue. He was lying very still. Maybe he was just stunned from the fall. If I was fast on my feet, maybe I could bring him the help that he needed?

I ran back toward the hospice, as fast as my legs could carry me. I met Brothers Gaston and Martin as they came down the path, following my paw prints. I barked loudly.

"You've found him, Barry?" Brother Martin asked.

I spun around and ran, leading them back to the gorge. I arrived before they did and licked Michel's face. But even then I knew it was too late. That face would never be pink and lively again. What I was after, if you want to know the truth, was a final taste of my good friend. When I had gotten it, I lifted my nose to the sky and howled.

The brothers came slipping and sliding down the side of the gorge, the sled banging clumsily along behind them. Their eyes were full of fear.

Skidding to a stop beside Michel, they fell to their knees. Just like me, they knew they were too late to save him. They dropped their heads into their hands and wept.

Afterward, they bound Michel's body on to the sled and hauled it up the side of the gorge and back to the hospice. It was a slow, sad trip. When they saw us coming, all of the men and all of the dogs came pouring out of the hospice to greet their fallen brother.

Later, Prior Louis allowed me to enter the chapel, where the men were saying their final farewells to Michel. Candles burned and the clerics sang. I raised my voice and joined in. This surprised them a little, I think. For a moment, they stopped singing and just stared at me: the dog singing in the clerics' chapel. Then, one by one, they took up their song again and we all sang together, each in his own fashion. In the flickering candlelight, I saw tears glistening in the men's eyes. They say that dogs don't shed tears the way humans do, but that evening my big canine heart wept.

Michel was my master, my teacher, my friend, my brother. And I had lost him.

A Big Misunderstanding

For the rest of the winter, the heavy snows did not let up. We had little time to mourn Michel's passing. Once again, the name Napoléon was the talk of the dining hall. Apparently the battle at the foot of the mountains had continued to rage. Everyone except Napoléon was sick and tired of it. The mountains were crawling with families whose homes had been destroyed by the war. There were also many young men who were running away from having to serve in the Little Colonel's army.

On our daily forays along the path, we often came across these young men. They were starving and usually dressed in rags. We brought them back to the hospice, where the clerics cared for them, just as they would any other traveler in distress. War was not our business. Rescue was. Once we had fed them and given them warm clothes, many of these young men did not want to leave. They wanted to hide out from Napoléon in the hospice. But they had to go, the clerics explained to them gently as they sent them on their way. They needed to make room for new travelers in need of warmth and comfort.

Those days, it seemed I spent as much time sleeping as I did awake. And I have to admit that, as at home in the snow as I had always been, sometimes the cold crept into my bones and made me just a little bit achy. The only thing for it was to lie by the fire. As I lay on the hearth one day, I heard the brothers say that I had earned my rest. They said that I had rescued over forty people. I wanted to tell them that I was not done yet! I was ready and willing to rescue another forty. I just needed a little rest and warmth. I was drifting off when something—I cannot say exactly what—woke me up. I lifted my head and cocked an ear.

Outside, all was still. Yet I knew in my bones that Something was coming. I put my head back down. A part of me dozed while the other part stayed alert, waiting for the distant thunder of the avalanche to come. When it did, not twenty minutes later, I leapt up and ran to the front door and scratched. Brother Martin let me out.

"Off you go, Barry," Brother Martin said. "I pity the poor devils who got caught in that slide.

Don't worry, old boy. We won't be far behind you."

Old boy? Who was he calling old boy? I was the match of any dog at the hospice and I was eager to prove it.

The avalanche had finished rumbling and all was silent again. So you might wonder how I knew where to go. Just as I sensed an avalanche coming, I also sensed where it had happened. And I headed for that spot as fast as I could go. I might no longer have been a puppy, but my legs and hips were still strong. I churned my way across the debris of the avalanche, nose to the ground.

I homed in on the scent right away. I detected one man trapped beneath the snow. My nose told me that he was not buried very deeply. Surely, I could uncover him all by myself. By the time the clerics arrived on the scene, I would have the man out of the snow and ready to be put on a sled.

Wouldn't the clerics be pleased with me!

I dug down until I reached his head. It was then I saw that he was not much older than a boy. He was hatless, and his hair and face were clotted with ice and snow. He was very cold, but he was alive. I licked the lumps of ice and snow off his face and felt the warmth returning to his skin. He stirred but did not yet open his eyes. I began to dig his shoulders out. The stirring grew to a thrashing as he tried to free himself with no help from me. There was something about the way he was moving that worried me. He was fighting me rather than working with me. Perhaps it was best for me to stand by and wait until the clerics arrived. But I still needed to do my job, so I lay by the traveler's head and snuggled. The bari hug would keep him warm.

Suddenly, his eyes snapped open and he stared

at me in terror. What was wrong with the boy? What frightened him so?

"Help!" he screamed.

Help? What was he talking about? I *was* helping. I was snuggling. Snuggling is something that we bari dogs do very well. But the boy kept on screaming so loudly that I feared he might set off an avalanche. So I leaned against him harder, hoping the warmth of my body would calm him until the clerics arrived. But still he screamed and carried on.

Finally, after much struggle, he managed to free his arms from the snow. In one hand he gripped something shiny and sharp. He raised his arm and drove the sharp thing into my body. It was a knife—like the kind the marronniers used in the kitchen! I growled at him, and then yelped in agony as he plunged the knife into my furry chest, again and again.

The clerics ran toward us, shouting as they came. One of them knocked the knife out of the boy's hand. The snow was splattered bright red with my blood. The very sight of it made me feel weak. My head began to spin. My legs buckled beneath me. How would I ever get back to the hospice?

"Get him!" the young man gasped, pointing at me. "That wolf tried to kill me."

"Hush, now," said Brother Martin as he and Brother Gaston pulled the boy out of the snow and tied him to the sled. "There is no wolf. There is only Barry. And Barry is a good dog."

"You're lying. He's a wolf and he tried to eat me!" the boy cried.

A wolf? The boy thought I was a wolf! If I

was anything other than a dog, I was a bear, and a tame one at that. I did not eat people. I saved them. But this boy was too cold and too frightened to understand. He was out of his mind.

My blood kept pouring out as the boy lay on the sled and raved. The brothers turned away from him and looked at me with great worry in their eyes. They moved quickly, packing snow into my wounds and binding me up with strips of cloth. Then, grunting with the effort, they lifted me and placed me on the second sled. They even wrapped a wool blanket around me. I could not believe this was happening. Barry the rescue dog was himself being rescued!

When we got back to the hospice, they carried me to one of the rooms. Someone had pulled the mattress off the bed and they laid me out on the floor. By now, my wounds had begun to throb and

my nose felt hot. The clerics bent over me, murmuring words of comfort. Gently, they washed my wounds with warm water and soap. I yelped and tried to hold my body still but my jaws snapped at the air. I wanted to bite the pain and make it run away. Such pain I have never felt before.

"This will dull the pain. Poor Barry dog," said Prior Louis.

He put a small black bitter-tasting pellet on my tongue. I gagged. Brother Martin held my jaws shut and stroked my throat until I swallowed it. After a while, the pain in my wounds lessened. I leaned back on the mattress. And I dropped off to sleep like a rock off the edge of a precipice.

I dreamed. In the dream, Mother came to me. Mother had passed away six years ago, but she stood by my mattress, as large as life. She rubbed her cold, wet nose against my hot, dry one. *Poor Barry,* she said. *What did that bad boy do to you?*

He did not mean it, I told her. *He was scared and cold and confused and not at all in his right mind. I forgive him.*

You are a big-hearted dog, Barry, Mother said.

After a while, I said, *Mother, it hurts.*

Yes, I know it does, my sweet son. You are very badly wounded. But I also know you are not ready to join me. You must sleep and heal and return to life.

Soon, Mother went away. Every time I opened my eyes, I found at least one cleric kneeling by my bed, watching over me. Sometimes there was more than one and they would speak in soft voices so as not to disturb me.

"Will he make it?" one of them asked.

"There is no telling," said the other. "The wounds are deep and he is no longer a pup."

I was too weak to climb to my feet and prove to them otherwise. I was too weak to sit up and lap water from a bowl. They had to squeeze water from a cloth onto my tongue.

Day by day, with the help of the men and my powerful will to go on living, I got better. Soon, I was able to return to my beloved corner in the cellar. There I could stand to eat and lap water from a bowl. But I still had to do my business in the straw. In this respect, it was like being a puppy. And, like a puppy, I was still not strong enough to venture outside. One of the young females named Heloise had whelped while I was healing. Her puppies squirmed in a pile across the room.

They are beautiful pups, I told her.

Heloise lay back as the pups suckled. I could tell she was very proud.

Every day, as the pups got bigger, I grew stronger. The little balls of brown and white fluff came over to bat my nose with their fat, little paws. I watched them wrestling, just like I had wrestled with Jupiter and Phoebe. Outside, I could smell dirt and green things. I could hear the sound of water dripping off the roof. The snow was melting.

One day, Brother Martin came to fetch me. I climbed to my feet and wagged my tail. Were we going out to rescue people? But when I stepped outside, I saw that there was no more snow. Spring had come while I was healing. After that, I came outside every day to sit on a blanket by the door and watch the birds and the hares. This was how I spent my days, watching spring turn to summer for however brief a time it visited before the snows returned.

On a warm summer's day when there wasn't a cloud in the sky, Brother Martin brought out the new puppies. I watched them discover the world as once my brother and sister and I had.

One of them, a pup named Phaistos, came up to me.

Do you want to play, old man? he asked.

Not today, little one, I told him.

Is it true that you are a hero? he asked, wagging his tail.

It is true I am a dog who does his job, I said.

Mother says you are a hero. She says you rescued more than forty people and fought a bear and saved the hospice from masked robbers.

Some of that is true, but not all of it, I told young Phaistos.

Mother speaks only the truth, Phaistos said. *She said you are a living legend and I have to be respectful.*

I am not a legend, I said. *I am just a dog who loves his job.*

I want to be just like you when I grow up, said Phaistos.

But when the first snows began to fall and the clerics made ready their sleds and their winter clothing, Brother Martin came to me.

"Barry," he said, "there is a kind and gentle man from down in the valley. He has heard of your plight. He has said he will take you to live with him."

Why was I leaving the hospice?

"Don't look so worried, Barry. He has a beautiful house and I am sure you will be very happy there."

I didn't understand what was happening, but I did understand this one important thing: my days of rescuing travelers were at an end. I, Barry the Rescue Dog, was retiring from active duty.

RETIRED FROM DUTY

The Gentle Man had traveled through the Great Saint Bernard Pass on several occasions. Each time, he had stayed at the hospice and seen with his own eyes what the rescue dogs did. He had heard stories about me, about the little boy I had saved, and about the bigger boy who had mistaken me for a wolf and tried to kill me. When he learned how badly I had been hurt, he sent word to the clerics that, in exchange for their kindness to him in the past, he would be happy to take me to live with him.

I traveled down the mountain with some merchants who were on their way to the city of Bern. We traveled at first on foot and then by cart. I was grateful when one of them put up a ramp and told me to climb in the back of the cart. I must admit that my bones creaked and my old wounds ached with every step of that downhill trek. And though the cart jostled me, it delivered me apace to my new home.

How noisy the city was! There were so many people. Far more than I had seen even on the busiest days at the hospice. There were men and women and children. There were horses pulling wagons. In the past, all I had known of the world of people were the hospice and the grounds. Here there was house after house, all looking alike with a forest of chimneys on top puffing smoke into the sky. There were chapels with bells, and market-places filled with wagons and horses and people who were shouting and laughing. And the smells! Hundreds of them wafting in the air. My nose quivered constantly.

We came to a neat stone house, one in a long row of similar-looking houses. It had three front steps and a small porch with a garden in front. A man stepped onto the porch and greeted us.

"Welcome to your new home, Barry," the Gentle Man said.

I climbed down from the cart and sniffed his hand. He had a good smell. I sniffed around the garden. I lifted my leg and let it be known that this was my home now. I followed the Gentle Man up the stairs and into the house.

The floors of the hospice had been bare stone and wood. Here the floors were of polished wood covered in places with soft woolly rugs. There were soft things to lie and sit on. The Gentle Man said to me, "These are not for dogs. You must not climb up onto the furniture, Barry."

He need not have worried. The floor had always been good enough for me. And, besides, with my old bones, I probably could not have made it up onto the furniture, anyway.

The Gentle Man showed me my bowls by the back door, near the kitchen. He fed me right away. I was hungry and thirsty from the journey. The food was good. Fresh meat mixed with meal. The water was clean and cold. Later, the Gentle Man took me out for a walk.

At first, I did not understand why I could not run ahead and lead the way, as I had with the clerics on the mountain paths. But the city was crowded and the streets were confusing. I was glad when the man hooked a leash to my collar and kept me near him. I understood that my place was close to the Gentle Man, at the other end of the leash. There was so much to see on our walk. There was grass and flowers and more trees than I had ever seen

before in a place that the Gentle Man called the Park. There were lots of choice spots in the Park where I could lift my leg and let this city know that Barry now lived there.

There were other big dogs like me in the Park. We approached each other and sniffed carefully.

They smelled like city dogs. There were small dogs
riding in carriages on ladies' laps who saw me and
yipped at me so fiercely I had to snort. What did
they think they were going to do to me with their
tiny little teeth and bodies not much bigger than
hares? Tear me limb from limb? There were birds,

too, and long brown things the Gentle Man called squirrels. I had half a mind to chase after them, but there was the leash to hold me back, and, besides, my running days were over. These were my plodding days, and I was at peace with that. They were sitting days, too, and I was content to sit with the Gentle Man while he read his newspaper. He took me to the Park every day.

Many people came to the house to visit with the man. Some of them came just to see me. The Gentle Man would greet them at the door. They would enter the house and approach me where I liked to lie on the woolly rug in the parlor in a shaft of sunlight. Usually the visitor was a mother or a father bringing their children to meet me. They would kneel down and stroke my coat. They would pat my head and offer me treats and coo over me.

"This is the world-famous Barry der Men-schenretter," the parents would explain to their children. There was such pride in their voices. It was as if I were their very own dog.

I bet that you have been wondering all this time what the *Menschenretter* part of my name means. Well, I will tell you, just in case you have not already guessed. It means "lifesaver" in the German tongue. To my visitors, to the world, that was who I was: Barry the Lifesaver.

"He saved forty people," they said.

"He saved a baby," they said.

"He saved the clerics from robbers who wanted to steal the silver cross in the chapel," they said.

I might have saved forty people. Frankly, I did not know. I had long since lost count. But as I have said, by the time I was born, there were not many robbers roaming the Alps. Still, I suppose that is what happens when you become a legend. People like to tell stories about you, and they don't always care whether the stories are the exact truth. That was all right with me. I knew who I was and what I had done. I had saved lives. I had rescued people from the White Death. And in the end, I had escaped the White Death myself.

In the Park, the Gentle Man had a favorite bench where he liked to sit and read. Lying stretched out at his feet, I could see beyond the trees of the Park and the city chimneys to the high peaks of the snow-covered Alps. On cloudless days, if I looked very hard, I imagined I could even see the roof of the hospice, glinting in the sunshine. How I missed the hospice. The Gentle Man was good to me, but I missed the clerics and the marronniers and the other working dogs. And, oh, how I missed the snow!

Then one morning, I woke up to see a familiar soft grayness in the sky out the window of my new home. It was not long before they came drifting down from on high, my dear old friends, the snowflakes. I went to the front door and scratched.

The Gentle Man said, "Would you like to take a walk in the snow, Barry?"

He might have been a new friend, but he already understood me so well. He attached the leash to my collar and together we went out for a walk in the snow. I plodded a little way down the street before I opened my mouth and felt the cold flakes melting on my tongue. I could smell the snow, which lightly covered all the other city scents. Later that afternoon, the Gentle Man took me out again. By that time, the snow in the Park had gotten deep. It was not as deep as the snow in the Great Saint Bernard Pass. But it was deep

enough for my purposes. I went down on my back
and rolled in it, just like I had when I was a pup.

I might have been a city dweller, living far away
from the place where I was born and had lived
most of my life, but I would always be a Dog at
Home in the Snow.

APPENDIX

More About the Saint Bernard

History of the Saint Bernard

Today, dogs like the Saint Bernard and the Great Dane have been bred for size and have reached nearly monstrous proportions for a dog. We know from bones that in ancient times even "big" dogs were not much bigger than a German shepherd. When Roman soldiers crossed the Alps to conquer the people of northern Europe over 2,000 years ago, they left behind what were, for their times, big dogs. These dogs, which the Romans called Molossers (but which we know as mastiffs), had fought side by side with the Roman legions and were pitted against lions in Rome's Colosseum. Because these big dogs ate a great deal, only armies and wealthy people could afford to own them.

The Great Saint Bernard Hospice was founded in 1049. No one knows when dogs came to live there, since a fire in 1555 destroyed all records. But there is a painting of a rescue dog hanging on the hospice wall that was done in 1695. The first dogs were probably gifts to the Augustine clerics and the nonreligious workers, known as marronniers. The clerics and marronniers must have led a lonely life in the mountains, and the dogs were probably intended as companions.

But after the dogs settled in they proved their worth as good watchdogs and workers. They helped the clerics haul supplies from the town of Bourg-Saint-Pierre up the mountainside to the hospice. They carried milk and cheese packed on sleds or in pouches from the stable to the hospice. Most importantly, they showed a talent for guiding people through snow and fog and finding lost travelers. The hospice workers called the dogs *baris* ("little bears" in Swiss German) because of their burliness and their hardiness in the snow. The baris quickly became famous for their rescue work. Although the baris were shown in paintings and newspaper engravings wearing barrels of brandy strapped around their necks, the baris offered the warmth of their bodies, not liquid refreshment, to the travelers they rescued.

In the 1800s, Napoléon marched his army across the Alps. The dogs and hospice workers helped the soldiers as they struggled to haul their cannons over rocky crags and crevices. General Desaix, one of Napoléon's favorite generals, so admired the bari dogs that when he died in battle,

Napoléon had him buried at the hospice.

The dog known as Barry was born at the hospice in 1800, the year of Napoléon's crossing. Barry distinguished himself by making more than forty rescues in snow and fog. Accounts of Barry's exploits vary. Some accounts say that he saved closer to one hundred people. Stories tell how he saved a little girl in the cave instead of a boy. Or that he died when another boy he tried to rescue attacked him with a knife. Barry's stuffed body can still be seen in the Natural History Museum in Bern. And there is a Barry monument at the dog cemetery near Paris.

Today, the Saint Bernard is no longer used for mountain rescue. German shepherds replaced Saint Bernards in the early 1900s, and German shepherds were, in turn, replaced by Belgian sheepdogs, Labrador retrievers, and flat-coated retrievers, all of whom have fewer problems with their hips. Highly trained search and rescue teams have replaced the clerics and marronniers of yesteryear.

In the 1850s, a Swiss man named Heinrich Schumacher so admired the alpine rescue dogs that he began to breed them. Working closely with the clerics, he was responsible for founding the breed as we know it today. He made a careful study of Saint Bernards. The more similar the dogs were to Barry, he felt, the more desirable they would be. But other breeders, feeling that the dogs could be improved if they had heavier coats, had, as early as the 1820s, begun to breed Saint Bernards with Newfoundlands. Heavier coats, they reasoned, would keep the Saint Bernard even warmer. But the heavier coats that resulted caused snow to stick in their fur, making the dogs too cold! Other breeders wanted to make Saint Bernards bigger.

Bigger, they reasoned, was better. So they crossed them with Great Danes and other oversize dogs. But like many oversize dogs, these animals often had trouble with their hips and hindquarters.

The first dog show to feature Saint Bernards was held in Switzerland in 1871. People from around the world marveled at the dogs. And in 1888, Saint Bernards officially came to America when they crossed the Atlantic Ocean, and the Saint Bernard Club of America was founded.

The Foundation Barry du Grand Saint Bernard still breeds dogs at the hospice. Their mission is to keep alive the Saint Bernard breed as it was embodied by Barry, as a living monument, free of the shifting and often extreme trends of breeders and hobbyists. The foundation makes sure that there is always a dog named Barry in residence, as there has been since the days of the original Barry. In the winter months, the dogs are moved down from the hospice to Martigny, where winters are less severe.

For more information, visit:

- nmbe.ch/research/vertebrates/research/kynologie/swiss-dog-breeds/saint-bernard-dog
- saintbernardclub.org/2008redesign/about_saints.htm
- smithsonianmag.com/history-archaeology/st-bernard-200801.html

The hospice still welcomes visitors. For one traveler's account, visit:

- snowshoemag.com/2012/03/03/col-du-grand-saint-bernard-hospice-a-night-with-the-monks

Or visit the official site for the foundation at:

- fondation-barry.ch

(Note: Click on the United Kingdom flag so the site appears in English.)

The Great Saint Bernard Hospice

The remounted Barry (1923). For over fifty years, this Barry wore a little barrel around his neck. It was removed in 1978 by the director of the Natural History Museum in Bern because there is no evidence that any dog from the hospice actually wore such a barrel. Barry was given back his barrel, however, in 2000, on the occasion of his two hundredth birthday. New research revealed that the 1923 remount had so altered his outer appearance that he might as well wear the legendary keg, too!

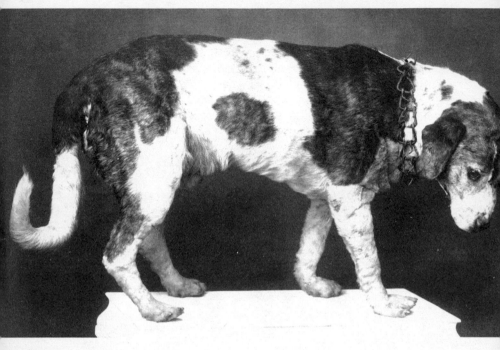

The first stuffed Barry (1814)

The Saint Bernard Today

The Saint Bernard is a big dog, part of the mastiff group. Its average weight is between 140 and 180 pounds. Its height at the withers, or shoulders, is about twenty-six to thirty inches. Its coat can be short- or long-haired and is white with red or brown patches and black shading around the face. The muzzle is square, the eyes are big, the ears are floppy, and the tail droops. Usually, the Saint Bernard's eyes are brown, but some have pale blue eyes.

Barry was not as big as the standard modern-day Saint Bernard. He probably weighed about one hundred pounds and would have been about twenty-five inches at the shoulder.

If you want to find out more about Saint Bernards, visit these sites:

- akc.org/breeds/saint_bernard/index.cfm
- saintbernardclub.org

There are rescue groups that specialize in finding homes for Saint Bernards whose owners can no longer take care of them. For more information, check out the following site: saintrescue.org.

Owning a Saint Bernard

Owning any dog is a big responsibility, but Saint Bernards are *big* dogs. While they don't necessarily require big yards, they take up a lot of space in a room and in a home. They are gentle giants and easy to train, but if you are interested in owning one, think about it very carefully. If you go to a Saint Bernard breeder, ask to meet the parents of the adorable pups. Get an idea of the parents' size. With the owner's permission, take one of the big bruisers around the block for a walk. If possible, groom a Saint Bernard. It will give you some idea of what a big job it is just keeping its fur spiffy. Getting a Saint Bernard into the backseat of a car is no small feat, either. They drool, and both short- and long-haired varieties shed.

And then there is the reason why, in older times, only the rich owned Saint Bernards: food. Dogs are fed according to their weight. A 180-pound healthy Saint Bernard eats about six to eight cups of dry food per day. And don't forget that the more food a dog takes in, the more poop comes out the other end. Scooping the poop of a Saint Bernard is not a chore for the faint of heart. But remember— Saint Bernards are sweet and gentle, and with a Saint Bernard, there's more dog to love.

For more information about owning a Saint Bernard, visit:

- saintbernardclub.org/2008redesign/new tosaints/new2saints.htm